'The story is set in Eugene McCabe's Monaghan homeland,
where Cyril, a sad little red squirrel .... ost his
parents and is now left .... unately
he takes the sound adv........ o tells
him to go out into the b........ dland,
field and fairy for........

CYRIL

The author: Eugene McCabe was born in Glasgow in 1930
and now lives on a farm in Co. Monaghan. He is the prize-
winning author of plays, fiction, and television drama. He
adapted Thomas Flanagan's novel, *The Year of the French*, for
Irish and French television. *Heritage and Other Stories* was
published by The O'Brien Press in 1985.
Cyril, The Quest of an Orphaned Squirrel, is his first story for
children.

The illustrator: Al O'Donnell, born in Dublin, is the Senior
Graphic Designer in RTE.

CYRIL

The Quest of an Orphaned Squirrel

Eugene McCabe

illustrated by
Al O'Donnell

LUCKY TREE BOOKS
THE O'BRIEN PRESS

First paperback edition published 1987.
First published in hardback 1986 by The O'Brien Press
20 Victoria Road, Dublin 6, Ireland.

British Library Cataloguing in Publication Data

McCabe, Eugene
Cyril: the quest of an orphaned squirrel. — (Lucky tree books, ISSN 0790-3669)
I. Title   II. Series
823.914 [J]   PZ7

ISBN 0-86278-131-0

The O'Brien Press acknowledges the assistance of
The Arts Council/An Chomhairle Ealaíon, in the
publication of this book.

10 9 8 7 6 5 4 3 2

Book design: Michael O'Brien
Editing: Íde O'Leary
Typesetting: in Andover by Phototype-Set Ltd.
Printing: Brough, Cox & Dunn Ltd.

Contents

For Patrick, who lived.

Preface

Years ago I saw a solitary red squirrel in a beech copse near my house, looking very forlorn. I never saw it again. Like the fox our children once saw running across the frozen lake at Burdantien, it was an image that stayed in my mind.

Years later it surfaced at a time of family stress (our son Patrick had been moved from Monaghan Hospital to Jervis Street, Dublin, after three operations, and was for a while gravely ill). Patrick recovered, and afterwards *Cyril* was written as a kind of therapy and 'thank you'.

Louis Lentin read it and an abridged version was broadcast in six parts on RTE, read by my daughter Ruth.

Here now, ten years later, is the full text.

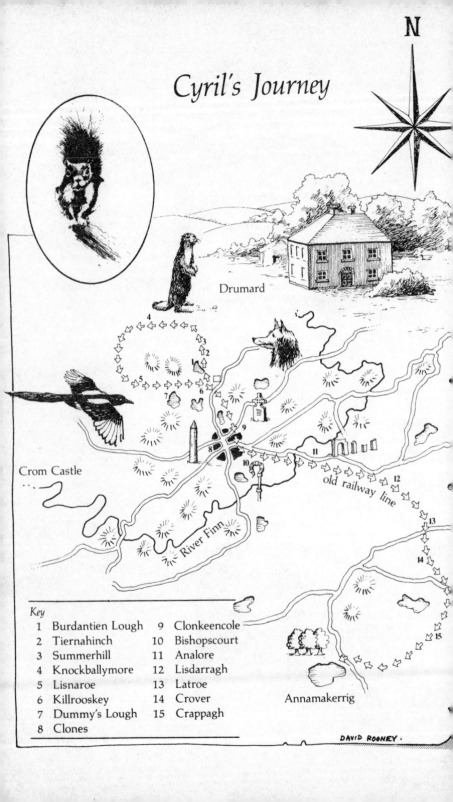

Cyril's Journey

N

Drumard

Crom Castle

old railway line

River Finn

Annamakerrig

Key
1 Burdantien Lough
2 Tiernahinch
3 Summerhill
4 Knockballymore
5 Lisnaroe
6 Killrooskey
7 Dummy's Lough
8 Clones
9 Clonkeencole
10 Bishopscourt
11 Analore
12 Lisdarragh
13 Latroe
14 Crover
15 Crappagh

DAVID ROONEY.

1

The Quest

IT WAS ALMOST DAWN. Late September. Though half asleep in
his drey, Cyril could sense the approach of day. He could tell
from two things — the angle of the light and the clamour of
nearby crows. At first glimmer they would begin their raucous
cawing, and most mornings two young ones would come
gliding over to perch above him, joking and mocking.

He could hear them now as they flapped from branch to
branch, taunting him:

'Little Cyril lives up high,
Alone, alone; we hear him cry.'

Unkind neighbours, Cyril thought. More than that — cruel,
really.

For, last October his parents had left the beech wood at
Drumard and gone to the townland of Knockballymore where
there were magnificent oak trees laden with acorns. Cyril had
been too small to travel. They had not returned. Two days
passed, then four, then six, then one week, two weeks, three
weeks, and then the leaves had turned from green to yellow,
brown and gold. Suddenly it was November. In three days
almost every leaf had gone and Cyril was alone in the great
bare crown of beech, staring across Burdantien Lough and
Summerhill Lough to the Dummy's Lough, and beyond that to
the beautiful lough of Knockballymore, through the sky-
drenching rains, with cold, dark winds from the west.

In the ten townlands round about there was no other family
of red squirrels. Cyril was an orphan. The winter had been
long, hard, lonely; the summer busy; and now almost a whole
year had passed and it was September again — early Lammas
floods spilling over lake and river bottom lands; cattle,
hockdeep, plodding to higher ground; swallows in their

hundreds on telephone lines, aware of the coming darkness and dreaming of the light of Africa. Soon they would be gone. Where could he go? Would he have to spend another winter here with no company but cold lakes and bare drumlins?

He opened his eyes and looked out over the top of his grass-lined drey. Through the lower escape hatch he could see the greeny-grey lichen on the beech trunks, and the floor of the wood scattered with brown and yellow leaves.

'Little Cyril lives up high,
Alone, alone; we hear him cry.'

Young crows were very foolish, Cyril thought. They wanted him to suddenly leap from his nest and jump at them. They liked to be frightened.

He stretched the forefingers on each of his paws and moved his thumbs, then straightened his five sharp toes. Slowly, he uncurled his long, round, bushy tail. It was glossy, and the colour of dark copper. He crept to the escape hatch. The two young crows were above him. They did not see him come out. Crouching in the fork of a branch under his nest he could hear them chattering and mocking.

'If he's all that lonely why stay here?'

'He's lazy, that's why. Asleep all winter. Then all summer plundering and storing.'

Cyril could not see them yet. He knew from the sound exactly where they were sitting. He crept out on a branch, filled his lungs with air, then shot, feet spread, across a high open space, curled his tail around a branch and slung his body up ten feet, sailing between the two crows, who fell, flapping with sudden, laughing squawks. Blinking, he watched as they cackled insults. They hated squirrels. Strange, he thought, how creatures who lived by thieving and plundering were so quick to condemn the same things in others. He watched them float down towards the house — a white, four-square house with a basement.

In the beech wood where Cyril lived there were about a hundred trees, some over two hundred years old. Behind the house there was a square yard of stone outbuildings, and behind that a kitchen garden with seven apple trees, two plum trees and one pear tree. There were other delights — loganberries, strawberries, blackberries, gooseberries, and

raspberries. It was the apples he liked best. Sometimes he split them and ate the seeds.

He was thinking of nipping down for an apple when, away to his right, high in the beech trees, there was a great commotion among the crows. Cyril watched, trying to hear what the argument was about. He knew a little crow language. There seemed to be about six warning words: watch, gun, food, man, cat, death. He had heard all these words until he was tired hearing them. But what he had never heard before was all the crows cawing the word 'death' together. This, now, was the only word that seemed to emerge from the argument. Then he saw eight crow cocks in a circle, and in the middle an old crow.

For weeks, Cyril had watched the old crow. Ten trees away he sat in a high branch, night and day, staring at the country-side. He had a damaged wing and was blind in one eye. Now and then the other crows swooped around him, mocking his age and defects. When they did this the old crow sat perfectly still and silent.

Now they were all around him, cackling loudly. Then there was a sudden silence. One by one the eight crows nodded at each other. Suddenly they jumped on the old crow, and then all fell, flapping and squawking to the ground, pecking without mercy. In less than half a minute the eight flew up and left the old, blind crow lying dead. A tabby cat came padding out from the yard and walked off with the dead crow.

Cyril was shocked. He stared down at the spot where the crow had lain. He shivered in fear and felt more lonely than ever. He longed to have someone who could explain things.

He thought of his friend Charlie, the badger. Charlie had told him about crow courts, but he had never seen one until now. To be killed by your own sort for some misdeed, defect, or for old age must be the most awful way to die, Cyril thought.

In the silence that followed the killing, Cyril sat, blinking gloomily. The crows were quiet. The sun had come out, the lake was a blinding shield, and somewhere a chainsaw began its hard, low moan as it clawed its way through the butt of a tree. No point in sitting on an old plough, brooding and feeling sad, Cyril thought. I'll go to Charlie. He thought again of the lonely winter ahead. How could he face that? Maybe Charlie would have some suggestions.

Charlie was said to be the wisest creature in ten townlands. Mention anything and he could talk about it. And everyone liked Charlie. He had a good mind, a good heart. Even the swans said that, and they praised hardly anyone.

When Cyril decided to move he moved very quickly. It was difficult to spot him except in the spaces between trees. In less than a minute he was sailing through the air, from branch to branch, through the great beeches down to the oak trees that grew beside the road, until he found himself at the chestnut whose forked trunk was the entrance to Charlie's sett.

Cyril did not leave the branch. Sometimes Fergus Fox lay hiding in the brown rushes close to Charlie's home; Cyril very much preferred to talk *down* to Fergus. Better to keep your distance with a sly fellow like that! He put his tongue against his teeth and gave a double whistle. Below the chestnut he heard a cough and a growl. Charlie was at home all right. He came out and peered up, his expression genial.

'Cyril, my dear little friend, how are you? Come on down. It's days since we had a talk.'

'How are *you*, Charlie?'

'So, so,' Charlie said. 'Not good, not bad — fair enough, I suppose. Can't complain, or shouldn't.'

'Anyone about?' Cyril asked.

'You mean Fergus Fox Esquire?'

'The very person,' Cyril said.

'Can't smell him hereabouts. No special odour in the soft air.'

Cyril dropped to the entrance to Charlie's sett. He somersaulted by way of greeting.

'You seem in good fettle, your usual high spirits,' Charlie said.

Cyril noticed that Charlie looked a little woebegone. He must have worries too, he thought. His eyes seemed bloodshot. He knew that Charlie was being kind when he talked of high spirits. Cyril had often told him about being sad and lonely. 'Yes, I'm fine — more or less,' Cyril said.

'Oh?'

'Well,' Cyril said, and told Charlie about the crow court.

Charlie looked away for quite a while, then said, 'Yes, seems cruel, heartless. But how would you like to be a hundred years old, half dead, sitting in a tree and dreaming of the barley fields of Louth and long ago? Not able to hunt. Maybe that killing was a kindness.'

'It was horrible,' Cyril said.

'Yes, life can be very ... 'Charlie searched for a word but couldn't find it.

Cyril heard Mrs B.'s voice from deep inside the sett, then the sound of small badgers wailing and caterwauling.

Charlie peered into the sett. 'Onset of winter, unsettling Mrs B. Then, of course, there's the dampness, and a lot of mouths to feed, and all kinds of rumours about trapping us and shooting us and hunting us and digging us out, and gassing us because some cows got sick maybe twenty miles from here — and we never travel more than two miles from home. Poor Mrs B. feels badgered. And so, in truth, do I.' He dropped his voice and nodded towards a hump of ground in the rushy bottom lands. 'I also understand,' he said, 'that "our friends" are about to tax the air we breathe.'

Cyril was so astonished that he did a double somersault and squeaked. 'How? Who? When? Where? Tax the air? Impossible! It's not fair.'

Charlie shrugged and sniffed and growled. 'A tricky question. A very clever move.'

Cyril watched Charlie's face and waited for explanation. He knew that when Charlie said 'our friends' he meant the rats who lived in the hump of high ground. The rats were very powerful, and feared by almost everyone. Charlie would never use as blunt a word as 'rat'. He always said 'our neighbours' or 'our friends in the hump'. The hump had been the dumping ground for the town slaughter-houses for over a hundred years. Now, although humans had stopped dumping, all the best rats for miles around continued to live there. At night they left it for the town dump over the hill and returned at dawn.

'How?' Cyril asked. 'They don't own the air.'

'Certain hints, suggestions; obscure remarks have been made. And, of course, they're everywhere — watching, listening, noting. There's nothing they don't know — when you come, when you go, when and where you eat, when you sleep, when and where you travel ... and when you die!

'Food is scarce for everyone, not only "our friends". Things have reached such a state, with hedges being rooted out,

dumps poisoned, rivers and lakes polluted, that "our friends" decided something would have to be done. They suggested that because of their eating habits they help to keep the air pure. So, they feel they have the right to tax us on the air we breathe — they keep our air clean, we pay them with food! Makes their life a lot easier, but ours even harder.'

'Rascals,' Cyril said.

'It seems,' Charlie said, somewhat mildly, 'an abuse.'

'What sort of tax?'

'I have been asked to leave a few potatoes, turnips, carrots, parsnips, apples, eggs or whatever I can manage every seven days. They make it sound a reasonable request. I'm a reasonable person, I hate unpleasantness with neighbours, especially "our friends".'

'Are you serious, Charlie?'

'I have no option, Cyril. I live on the ground. They can threaten me. Different for you, you live up in the trees. They can't catch you.'

'I'd refuse.'

'Not if you were me.'

'Are the swans paying?'

'They're leaving some food at the side of the stream between the two lakes.'

'And Fergus Fox?'

Charlie gave a deep chuckle. 'Fergus has said he'll deliver a turkey, half a dozen old hens, and an odd lamb for good measure. He made a speech that shamed the rest of us, full of generous gestures and promises. "Absolutely," he said. "You people do the dirty work and should be well paid."'

Charlie dropped his voice. 'The truth is, Fergus will never, ever, the longest day he lives, give them as much as a chicken's liver, and he will have marvellous excuses. He'll keep making promises, and they'll believe him, and by some miracle he won't suffer. Ah well, we're all different.'

'If I can help...' Cyril ventured.

'Not at all,' Charlie said. 'Tax is a fact of life. People who live honestly are plundered, and people who plunder everyone get away with murder. Same the world over.'

'I'll pay nothing,' Cyril said, 'but I'll snitch apples for you, Charlie.'

'It's too risky. Anyway, you can't swing around by yourself much longer up there. In a few weeks it'll be winter. Last winter was hard on you. You must be uncommonly, profoundly, unutterably lonely.'

'Yes,' Cyril said. This was what he had really come to discuss. He looked sideways, away towards the lake. The water dazzled. He knew he was near to tears. Charlie had a way of putting things that made you understand the truth, and the truth was that Cyril was very, very lonely. Charlie had this tax worry. All the other animals had worries too. But Cyril felt that loneliness was the worst thing of all.

Charlie broke the silence. 'The biggest temptation — and the thing to be avoided — is self-pity.'

'Self-pity?' Cyril repeated.

'Being sorry for yourself. It's a disease. Humans suffer from it — they drink out of bottles, fall down, fight and smash themselves because they think they have terrible problems. The truth is, there's nothing that can't be solved. Believe me, this is true.'

'I'm not so sure,' Cyril said.

'Your problem can be solved too,' Charlie assured him. 'You must travel, Cyril. You must set off on your own into the unknown until you find someone of your own kind. You must find a companion who will come back and share your beech wood. You squirrels can travel long distances. You're bound to hear of other squirrels. Don't brood and feel sorry for yourself. Go out into the world; search until you find what you want.'

Cyril sat, silent and thoughtful, after this speech. He was excited, too.

'It's a quest,' Charlie said.

'Quest?' Cyril asked. 'What's that?'

'To search without ceasing day and night, travelling the towns and townlands, through faraway fields, forests and fairy forts until you meet your true love. That's a quest. It is the most important thing you will ever do in your life.'

'Life's quest,' Cyril said, fascinated. 'But where will I go?' The world seemed large and threatening at that moment.

'You must make inquiries,' Charlie said. 'Find out which direction to take.'

'Who can tell me?'

'Ask the birds,' Charlie said. 'And the rabbits, pigeons, hares, foxes, crows, otters. Especially otters. Good travellers and they know all the secret ways. You might even consult "our friends". And then, of course,' Charlie paused, 'there are your grey cousins.'

Cyril spun around and his tail flicked angrily. 'Never!'

'But why not, Cyril?'

'I'm a different colour. I think differently. I look different. I feel different. I am different. And they're bullies. They mock and hiss and despise and chase me because I'm smaller. Grey squirrels are the last ones in the world I'd ask.'

There was quite a long silence before Charlie replied. 'You are closely related,' he said.

'They look,' Cyril said, 'a bit like "our friends".'

'That's not kind,' Charlie said.

'But it's true,' Cyril said. 'And you're forever talking about truth.'

Charlie sighed. 'The real truth is that there is great trouble between you red and grey squirrels. It could and should be solved.' Charlie paused, and looked so steadily into Cyril's eyes that Cyril was forced to look away. 'Think about that — and, before you go looking for your dream, remember that romance is like. . .'

Charlie paused for such a long time that Cyril asked, 'Like what, Charlie?'

'Have you seen the swans by moonlight?'

'Often.'

'The hare in snow?'

'Yes.'

'The kingfisher at Shannock?'

'Yes.'

'The orchards of Armagh in April?'

'I've heard of them.'

Charlie paused, and then said, 'They may not be what they seem.'

'I don't understand.'

'You will some day.'

'But romance, Charlie, — you haven't told me what it is.'

'I have hinted, suggested. Be careful of dreams. They may not come true. All I can say now is good luck, Cyril. Make your inquiries, go on your travels, and we'll talk again soon. Farewell, little friend.'

And Charlie went back into his sett. That was always how he ended a conversation — bluntly, leaving Cyril with a feeling that something had been left unexplained.

2

King Rat's Advice

NOW WHAT, CYRIL THOUGHT, OR WHERE? The September sun was gold, and filling the countryside; the ripeness of autumn was everywhere, nuts, fruits and berries galore. What had Charlie suggested? Talking to various people. Yes, that was it! The nearest were, as he called them, 'our friends', the rats. Why not give them a try? He dropped to the ground and went zig-zagging through clumps of rushes, then leapt straight to the top of a dead ash tree on a hump of high ground. No one about.

Cyril whistled through his teeth and a guard rat appeared at the base of the tree. He peered around cautiously. He seemed shortsighted. They were almost blind, Cyril remembered. He watched the guard sniff the air and then said, 'It's me — Cyril.'

'Ah,' the guard responded and looked up. 'How are you, Cyril?'

Cyril knew that the guard rat, in fact the whole rat colony, cared about nobody and nothing but themselves, but he answered cheerfully, 'Fine. How are you?'

'As well as can be expected. What do you want?'

'Information.'

'Of what sort?'

'Personal.'

'Nothing's private in this world. Tell me what you want and I'll ask the King.'

The manner was rude. Cyril decided to try again; rudeness from people you don't care about doesn't matter much. 'Can't you ask the King to have a word with me?'

The guard rat scratched his whiskers with a paw. 'Why?'

'Because I ask politely.'

'Humans are polite. So are dogs and cats and foxes. Politeness to us is nothing.'

'What have I ever done to you people?'

'You hate us, like everybody in the world.'

Cyril looked away to the beech grove up at the house. Hundreds of starlings had arrived there and were chittering. He didn't really hate rats — they filled him with dread. But he couldn't very well say that. He nibbled his claw and said, 'It's important.'

'To whom?'

'You, all of you. To your King.'

'I don't believe you.'

'You don't have to,' said Cyril.

The guard rat squinted up. Squirrels were neither here nor there. Living so high and obscure in treetops they were independent of everyone and everything, and untaxable. But perhaps this cheeky, big-tailed high-jumper had something to offer.

'You'll have to tell me,' the guard rat said.

'No,' Cyril said. 'I won't.'

There was a long pause. From the corner of his eye Cyril saw the guard rat slither towards the hole. In a clear voice, Cyril said: 'I'll wait two minutes. If the King doesn't come, I'll be gone.'

The guard paused to hear this, then vanished. In less than half a minute Cyril could hear a squeaky commotion deep in the mound, then silence. First the guard rat came out, then five other big grey-brown fellows, rough-haired and suspicious looking. Then, after a pause, King Rat. He was as grey as a beech trunk, very glossy and smooth, wrinkled under his neck, and his whiskers were longer and greyer than the others'. There were pouches under his bright and glittering eyes. His claws were longer also.

Without looking up, the King said, 'I will speak *up* to no one; if you have something to say come down and say it, face to face.'

'Of course,' Cyril said, and dropped lightly to within two yards of King Rat. He knew he could be at the treetop or ten feet away if any of them made a hostile move. Close up the King seemed even more impressive. He seemed bored and tired when he looked at Cyril. 'Well?'

'Your Majesty,' Cyril said.

'Don't mock,' King Rat said.

'I must call you something, Sir.'

'Say your piece and be done,' the King said. 'What's important to us?'

Cyril sniffed. 'This air tax?'

King Rat raised one eyebrow. 'Who told you?'

'Charlie.'

'Brother brock, our grave old crock! What did he say?'

'Quite a fair tax,' Cyril told him.

King Rat smiled. 'In two hours we could drill his burrow full of holes and his cubs would drown in the first downpour. Naturally, he's helpful.'

The King smiled, showing very white, pointed teeth. Not only hideous to look at, thought Cyril, but spiteful. As a friend of Charlie's he was tempted to say this, but it would be a waste of time. Anyway, he wanted information.

'Come on,' the King muttered, 'you didn't call me out here to talk about a tax that doesn't concern you.'

'I thought I might pay a portion of Charlie's tax.'

'How much?'

'An apple a day, when available.'

'A small luxury.'

'For me it's dangerous.'

'Dangerous! Who has ever caught a squirrel?'

'Cats and stoats. Dogs, foxes and hawks are all enemies. Humans, sometimes.'

'Not often.' The King fixed his glittering eyes on Cyril. 'You didn't call me out here to moan about that. What else?'

He was shrewd. Cyril could think of nothing else to say, so he muttered, 'Well ... eh ...'

'Go on.'

'It's a small problem.'

'Yours or mine?'

Cyril hesitated, then said, 'Mine.'

'Your problems don't interest us.'

The other six rats grinned and hissed. Cyril coiled to spring away to safety. The King put up a claw for silence and said, 'You've wasted three minutes of my day, I might as well hear you out.'

'I am an orphan.'

'So are millions.'

'There are no red squirrels within miles that I know of.'

The six guard rats sniggered. King Rat waved them away. They slunk off into the hole, grinning.

'You are asking me do I know any?'

'Yes.'

The King put his head to one side and looked away, then glanced back with one eye.

'What happened to your parents?'

'I don't know.'

After quite a silence the King said, 'I do.'

Cyril's heart jumped. His eyes filled with tears. 'You can tell me?'

'Nothing much to tell. They were caught in an orchard in a place called Knockballymore, three miles from here.'

'Caught? Are they alive?'

King Rat muttered: 'Shot. Pilfering apples. One barrel of a gun killed both.'

'How do you know?'

For quite a while the King did not reply. 'The bodies,' he said then, 'were full of lead.'

When Cyril realised how King Rat knew this he was filled with a sudden loathing and horror. Both his parents shot by humans, then devoured by rats in a remote townland. He didn't want to talk any more to the King. Now that he knew the manner of their death he felt sick. It would have been better not to know.

'Horrible,' he said quietly.

King Rat stared and gave a faint shrug. 'What's horrible to you is natural to us. And what is natural to you is horrible to us.'

'I do not do horrible things,' Cyril said, and he was trembling.

'You leap thirty feet across a space a hundred feet in the air. That to us is horrible — total nightmare.'

'I don't want to talk any more.'

'As you please,' the King said.

'Wait,' Cyril said, 'please.'

The King paused and turned.

'Do you know of any of my kind anywhere about?'

'Not near.'

'Anywhere?'

'Crom Castle, south-west of here. Pippin and his wife, Lily, have a daughter and three sons. There's another crowd at Annamakerrig — Old Falvey, the widower, has three daughters. That's south-east of here.'

'How do I get to Crom Castle?'

'West. Follow the river Finn.'

'And to Annamakerrig?'

'East. Follow the old railway line.'

It seemed to Cyril that both places were very far away.

'How far?' he asked.

'Half a week's journey for you. Maybe the swans would fly you down if they're not too busy shining their souls!' King Rat gave an odd little smile. 'You will deliver an apple each day?'

'When possible,' Cyril said.

King Rat disappeared below ground. Cyril took a very deep breath. The interview had been strange, both unnerving and fascinating. The odd thing was that although he was a very dreadful creature, and malicious, the King was in no way ashamed. You had to admire the cunning and the knowledge. Charlie had told him that rats were almost blind, poor runners and in most ways cowardly. But they were very persistent. They could claw their way through two feet of concrete; they could run up the side of a rough-cast house; dogs were wary of them, cats would never attack them head-on, and no matter how other animals and humans tried to destroy them, they managed to survive — and life, Charlie said, is mostly about staying alive, and 'our friends', he said often, do that very well.

And this was what Cyril was obliged to do now — to survive, to find a partner in true love. I must carry on with my quest, he thought. I'll go west to Crom Castle and find Pippin and Lily and their family.

3

Cedric and Cynthia

KING RAT HAD SUGGESTED consulting the swans. Because of the rushes and the sedge at the lake's edge Cyril could not see them now. Had they left their lake he would have heard the drumming clamour and creak of their great wings — and they had been on the lake ten minutes before. He would go over and have a word with them. Strange and difficult to talk to, most creatures said, but polite and helpful in a remote sort of way.

As he zig-zagged towards the lake he suddenly heard the crackle of dead rushes and a fearsome panting. He paused for a split second to look around. The heart twisted in his body from fright. In that flash he saw a huge black head, a red open mouth and the sharp, yellow teeth of a black labrador dog. He sprang sideways with a terrified squeak. The roadside hedge was too far and he could not now cut back to the dead ash tree. He was trapped.

In a panic he kept in line for the lake, leaping and bouncing this way and that. He was ahead of the black dog but only by a few yards. As he approached the lake he could see Cedric and Cynthia Swan poise their long necks at the approaching sounds. Neither seemed in any way startled. There was nowhere for Cyril to go. With one great leap he cleared the sedge and bulrushes at the lake's edge and splashed into the water. Then he realised that he had done the most stupid thing possible. He was tiny and swam very slowly. The black labrador was big and a powerful swimmer. He heard the great dog smashing and splashing through the sedge, then the massive black head was in the water, swimming strongly towards him. Cyril screamed in terror. This was the end. What a stupid way for a squirrel to die! The great mouth was about three feet away. Cyril kept swimming, his eyes closed, awaiting the awful smash, the sudden pain of death.

Suddenly there was confusion. Huge shadows overhead and splashes of black and white, strange pounding sounds, yelping, and a curious whirring noise. Was he dying or dreaming? He opened his eyes and looked over his shoulder to see Cedric Swan, huge above the water, his large black webbed feet as though he were standing on the surface of the lake, his enormous wings mercilessly beating the labrador's head. Twice the dog sank. Each time it surfaced Cedric followed, pummelling with majestic smashing blows, forcing the dog under again and again until he reached the reeds, stumbled out, and ran, yelping, away from the lough's edge towards the sloping scrublands of Killrooskey. Cyril watched the retreat, and realised that he was so shocked he could scarcely keep afloat. Suddenly he felt a gentle pressure on his neck. He was being lifted from the water. Then he was sitting, trembling, on the white feathers of Cynthia's back. She was craning her elegant neck and looking at him with great gentleness.

'You are a very foolish little fellow, are you not?'

'Yes, I am,' Cyril admitted, his teeth chattering.

'What on earth possessed you to leave those magnificent beech trees and go roaming about the open fields alone?'

Cyril tried to answer but he was shivering so much he could not.

'Shake the water from your fur and the sun and wind will dry you presently.'

Cyril did as he was told.

'Do you have a name?'

Cyril told her his name. She smiled. The lake was very still. As he shook himself, droplets sparkled, shimmering on the surface like diamonds. Gradually his heart slowed, his teeth stopped chattering. Cynthia looked away towards Cedric. He was still at the lake's edge, his feathers ruffled, his head high and angry watching the retreating labrador. Satisfied that all danger was past, he turned, composed his feathers and began paddling towards his spouse, who sat motionless, the red squirrel perched on her back. Cedric's expression seemed rather severe. He said: 'What were you thinking about, squirrel? The whole thing is most intrusive and interruptive.'

Very quietly, Cynthia said, 'I have spoken to him, dear. His name is Cyril.'

Cedric arched his head backwards, looked at Cyril steadily and then said quietly, *'Sciurus vulgaris.'*

Cyril could see that he was disguising a smile.

'Cyril, Cedric and Cynthia.' Cedric gave a little laugh and added, 'We're very fond of elegant language on this lake.'

'Oh,' Cyril said. Not very elegant, he thought.

'We like it especially when many words begin with the same letter.'

'Ah!' Cyril said, and did a somersault, landing neatly on Cynthia's back.

'Spirited and sprightly,' Cedric said. 'Now tell us what nonsense brings you to the dangers of foreign fields?'

Cyril told them his story: how his parents had died, what Charlie had advised, about his quest, what King Rat had told

him. The rest they knew. There was a long silence when he had finished. Cedric cleared his throat and muttered something, and Cyril noticed that Cynthia's eyes were glassy. Eventually, Cedric said, 'A most melancholy, sad and sorry tale.'

'Shattering,' Cynthia said.

'Sad and shattering,' Cedric said. 'The thing is, what to do now?'

Cyril said: 'This is my problem. I am trying to get to Crom Castle. I have not been very successful so far.'

'How can we advise him, Cedric?' Cynthia asked.

'I think, maybe, we should glide about a while and reflect a little. Do you reflect, Cyril? Commune?'

'Reflect?' Cyril asked.

'Reflection — is, oh — how shall I put it — the most important thing in life. If you have no time to reflect on what you are, where life is leading, you might as well not be living.'

'It's thinking,' Cynthia explained, 'or what some call communing with the great creature who rules the universe.'

'Do you believe in the great ruler, Cyril?'

'I don't know, Sir.'

'An agnostic!' Cedric said, frowning.

'An innocent,' Cynthia corrected.

They started to move slowly across the lake. The effect, Cyril thought, was almost miraculous. The still water and the sunlight were beautiful. They went gliding silently about ten feet from the lake's edge. Cyril, sitting on Cynthia's back, could see down through the clear water to masses of green undergrowth and hundreds of perch and roach darting in silvery shoals. Two curlews wheeled overhead with rippling calls, dropping suddenly into the marshland at Burdantien, an area of cut-over bog, alive with willow, stunted thorn bush, drumheads and coarse grass, alder trees and bog pools. In the middle of this, somewhere, the swans had their nest. From the treetops it often seemed to Cyril as if they were paddling silently through trees and grass.

'Nice sound,' Cyril said.

'What?' Cedric asked, absently.

'Curlews.'

'It's agreeable,' he said. 'A lovely, liquid note, but they have strange habits. This time of year they build maybe three or four nests which they don't use.'

'Why?' Cyril asked.

'Why do you sleep all winter?'

'I don't.'

'But surely...'

'I snooze. Some days I eat. Some days I even run around in the trees.'

'Are you sure?'

'I'm certain.'

'I always thought you people slept the winter long. Perhaps you merely dream of eating and running around?'

'Am I dreaming now?'

'No.'

'Then, I don't sleep all winter.'

'Do you do a little gathering?'

'No. Not 'till spring.'

'Some of your kind are inclined to rob nests.'

'I have never robbed a nest in my life,' Cyril said.

'Grey squirrels certainly do,' Cedric said.

'They are rats,' Cyril said, loudly, 'who climb trees.'

Cynthia asked, very quietly, 'Who told you that, Cyril?'

'My parents.'

Cynthia smiled and said: 'They are not rats. And even if they were, rats must live too.'

Cyril realised that his angry outburst about his grey cousins must appear narrow and ugly.

Cynthia said, 'We should be slow to judge others.'

'Yes,' Cedric said. 'It's easy to forgive faults in a friend, not so easy in enemies.'

They had gone floating past a pump-house and were now well up the lake near the new forest under the Bracken Hill. As they approached, the trees seemed to go floating backwards. When they reached the stump of a huge ash tree that had been pushed to the lake's edge, they faced the sun and Cedric began to commune:

> 'Lord of swallow-swoop and meadow crake,
> Of gripe and ditch, of quiet lake,
> Of wren and robin, crow and kite,
> Of sun by day and moon by night,

Maker of tides that never cease,
Master of stars — guard our peace.'

For ten minutes or more they went on communing. Cyril's pointed ears became more and more pointed as he listened. He had never in his short life heard anything like this. There was something about the swans that made him uneasy — he understood why Charlie spoke of them so respectfully. This must be what Charlie meant when he said they were high-minded. At the same time, Cyril felt there was something cold about Cedric. Swans were not much fun, but they knew how to deal with savage black dogs! There was quite a long silence after they had communed.

Cyril wanted to sneeze, but felt that if he did it would be a most serious matter. He put a finger and thumb on his nose and managed to prevent it. Eventually, Cedric asked, 'Do you think you could commune, Cyril?'

'I'd like to try.'

'Can you remember the words?'

'Not one.'

Cedric seemed a little displeased. 'You were listening?'

'Oh yes,' Cyril said, and sneezed suddenly.

'Poor little chap must be frozen,' Cynthia said.

'You must be conscious of creation and beauty,' Cedric said, unlistening. 'Living in those magnificent trees, you must be.'

'Every minute of every day,' Cyril said.

'Then you must try to commune.'

'But I do.'

'How?' Cynthia asked.

Cyril hesitated. What he was about to say might sound foolish, but he decided to say it just the same. 'When I'm happy and the day is fine, or nuts are in millions, I jump and swing and sail through the trees and laugh at nothing.'

'That is communing,' Cynthia said.

'I expect so,' Cedric muttered.

'But that was last year when my parents were alive,' Cyril said.

There was quite a silence, then Cedric said, 'Listen, Cyril, it has been most pleasant to meet and mull with you.'

'I'd be dead if we hadn't met,' Cyril said.

Cynthia laughed.

'Nothing happens by chance,' Cedric said. 'There is a hidden meaning in our meeting. We must talk again. Pursue your quest; it's a noble one. I wish you hearty happiness.'

'How will I get to Crom Castle?' Cyril asked.

Cedric blinked, looked away and said: 'Otters. Your friend badger's right, otters are your best bet. Tremendous travellers, from seashore to littlest lake. They know the sources, channels, underwater ways. Seek out the otters. They'll get you there. Meanwhile, I wish you success.'

31

'Thank you,' Cyril said, and felt those two words to be very poor stuff indeed. He wished he could think of something elegant to say. It was also clear to Cyril that it was less trouble for Cedric to make a speech than to help get him to Crom Castle! Small as he was, Cyril had his pride, and had no notion of asking the swans to oblige.

He bid the swans farewell with a blink and a nod, jumped from Cynthia's back to the tree stump at the lake's edge, and watched them float away across the lake, Cedric slightly ahead. Twice, Cynthia looked back, arching her beautiful neck in farewell. In response, Cyril jumped, thrusting his bushy tail up, waving it from side to side.

No wonder other creatures envied the swans their moonshaped lake in a hollow of drumlins with its fringe of birch and alder, and a mysterious silence over all but for the occasional curlew and winter guests from the north — teal and woodcock. Guard our peace, the swans had chanted. Selfish creatures, Charlie had once muttered. I suppose, Cyril thought, they found true love long ago; they don't need anyone or anything else.

4

Fergus Fox Esquire

IT WAS SHEER BLISS sitting there looking at everything — the lake, the other animals, the countryside. But that was not questing. Night and day, Charlie had said. Onwards, thought Cyril, and in a flash he had sprung from the lakeside tree stump to the top of a pine tree. The sun was high now, the lake a blinding mirror, the swans far off. A cool wind blowing across the water made brittle music in the sedge, swaying last year's ragged drumsticks, a reminder of winter. Behind him was the Bracken Hill. From the top of that hill he would be able to look towards the river. Perhaps he would spot his otter friend, Loughlin?

He set off, swinging and leaping through the pine trees. Below him was the brown floor of dead cones and pine needles. When the forest ended he skipped, running and jumping uphill for fifty yards to the cover of bracken and whins. He paused and peeped out — all clear. In less than half a minute he was high on a wild cherry tree looking across at the river.

The small, wild cherries were delicious. He ate a few, spitting out the stones as far as possible. He watched rabbits nibbling ten yards from the ditch below. How on earth, he wondered, could rabbits live all their lives on grass and herbs? How extraordinary the world was, and all the different creatures. Two pigeons flew high overhead. I expect, he thought, they think only flying creatures are free and have an interesting life. My high-flying leaps would seem very tame to swallows who fly thousands of miles. A deep thought. He gave a little laugh — a noisy, raucous sound that startled the grazing rabbits. I'm quite a clever fellow. But, I'm wasting time, he thought suddenly. The thing to do was to try to meet Loughlin.

Loughlin was a grey-whiskered otter who came from Lough Erne to fish this quiet tributary of the Finn river. She was, as everyone knew, wise about lakes, rivers and streams, and she knew the three hundred and sixty-five islands on Lough Erne, some small, some quite big, and most of them dense with oak, ash and thorn. Loughlin was good fun, too, even if she was sometimes slightly scatterbrained. Often she started talking about three or four things at the same time and in the end said nothing about any of them. A pleasant creature to be with. Casual about most things except waterways.

Cyril was about to drop to a lower branch and head off again when he suddenly heard the distant yelping of hounds from Tiernahinch, beyond Drumard. He had often watched the hunt with a mixture of fear and excitement. He caught sight of an orange flash in the woods, then suddenly it was in the open. Even though he was over half a mile away Cyril knew it was Fergus Fox, tail out like a flag, running easily down the sloping field. He crossed the road, went through a small area of scrub, then out into the lake field. For a while Cyril could not see him because of the ditch. Then he saw huntsmen coming up the field, yodelling and yahooing after the hounds. He knew they were watching Fergus, who emerged now at the end of the ditch. Without pause he leaped into the lake exactly as Cyril had done and swam steadily towards the forest. He was still swimming when the hounds came through the wood yelping and tonguing as they followed the scent. At the road they lost track, then one hound found it, gave tongue again and soon they were all running down the back of the ditch.

Cyril's heart began to pound. He did not trust Fergus Fox, but you had to admire him and wish him well. He could not see where Fergus was now, but knew that he must be out of the water and into the forest. He was still wondering where he might have gone when the orange flash came from the bracken fifty yards away. Fergus, dripping wet and not even running, came across the open part of the Bracken Hill, in no way worried or concerned. He stopped, sat on his hind legs and looked down at the hounds. There were about twelve of them, yelping and arguing among themselves, some running back towards the road, others going up the other side of the ditch. Eventually, the leader of the pack gave tongue and they all followed, running around the wrong side of the lake. From his perch in the cherry tree Cyril could see Fergus smiling.

He called out, 'Mr. Fergus Fly Foots, you fooled them again!'

Without looking around Fergus gave a little chuckle and drawled, 'It's you, Cyril, what brings you up here?'

'Cherries.'

Fergus sat for another full minute watching the countryside. The hounds were now out of sight. When he was sure that no strays had tracked him he came over and sat under the tree. He looked up at Cyril.

'Where did they find you?' Cyril asked.

'Near a henhouse at Gortnawinney.'

'Did you get any hens?'

Fergus ignored the question, smiled and asked, 'Can you see stray hounds from up there?'

Cyril scanned the landscape. 'None.'

'There's one old hound called Jason, never hunts with the pack — he knows a few of my tricks.'

'They're miles away now,' Cyril said.

'Mostly a stupid lot,' Fergus said. 'They make so much noise, and the humans running after them screaming and hollering are worse.'

'Are you ever afraid?' Cyril asked.

Fergus shook his head. 'With horses it can be a little scary. The humans can see where I go, and some horses can jump high and run very fast, but...' He shrugged and did not finish what he was going to say, so Cyril asked, 'Where are you staying at the moment, Fergus?'

'Here and there.'

'Charlie says you come and go.'

'You were talking to Charlie?'

'Yes.'

'When?'

'This morning.'

'How is he?'

'Worried a little.'

'He's always worried — what now?'

'This air tax.'

'Our filthy friends.' Fergus's lip twisted with contempt.

'They tell me,' Cyril said, 'that you have promised to pay.'

'They?'

'King Rat himself told me.'

'Charming creature. You spoke to him?'

'Yes.'

'Quite an honour.'

'Are you going to pay?'

'What do you think?'

'You won't.'

'Correct. If I can find poisoned lambs I will, of course, leave them quietly, compliments of Fergus Fox Esquire. Otherwise, they'll get nothing from me.'

'Would you do that, Fergus?'

'Of course. I hate them.'

'They must live,' Cyril suggested.

'They must die too — and the sooner the better.'

What a strange character he was, Cyril thought. Like the rats, you couldn't really like him, but you couldn't really hate him either. Clever animals were like that. He had heard cats talk in much the same way. They were cold and didn't care what anyone thought about them. 'Charlie's going to pay.'

'Fear,' Fergus muttered. 'I'm afraid of nothing but a gun.'

'If they bored holes around your den, your little ones might drown,' Cyril suggested.

'And what would I be doing while they were boring holes?' Fergus gave his long, pointed jaws a sudden snap. 'Quick as that! Charlie's too slow to bite back and he can't see as well as I can, or hear or smell.'

This boasting annoyed Cyril slightly. He knew it was not true, so he said, 'If they came in hundreds, what then?'

'I have many friends. I'd give one special bark and dispose of our tax problem very quickly.' Fergus smiled and looked up at the tree. 'Surely you're not paying, Cyril?'

'No, but I thought I'd help Charlie.'

Fergus nodded. Cyril knew that Fergus thought this a foolish gesture.

'It's a free world,' Fergus said, 'more or less.' He smiled up and asked: 'Do rats eat cherries? Are you gathering food for them up there?'

'I just happened to be here when I heard the hounds.'

'Why are you so far west?'

'I'm questing,' Cyril said.

'For what?'

'A red squirrel family.'

'Ah,' Fergus said, a paw on his head as though trying to remember. He tapped his skull gently. 'Would you care to come down, Cyril? We can talk more closely. I'm sure I could solve your problem. I take it you're lonely?'

'That's true,' Cyril said.

'Then come down here and we'll have a chat.'

'I can hear quite well up here,' Cyril said. 'Also, I can keep a look out for stray hounds. I don't want to see you eaten.'

'Very true,' Fergus said, 'very wise.'

What an old cute-nose Fergus was. Solve your problem! He wasn't lying. A squirrel for breakfast would solve two problems, Fergus's hunger and Cyril's loneliness.

'You're afraid of me, Cyril, aren't you?'

Cyril opened his mouth to reply but thought better of it.

'You are,' Fergus said. 'Most creatures are afraid and full of

hate. Next to rats I'm the most hunted creature in this whole land. My smell is disliked, my orangey, earthy coat and tail, my thin, pointy face. But I don't whine about it. I live by my wits, I love my family. If I'm cornered by a dozen savage hounds, I'll fight and die in silence. Those moony-looking swans — look at them floating about in grandeur — when it comes to dying they gobble like turkeys.'

'Don't they sing?'

'Gobble and squawk.' He paused, then muttered, 'I know.'

Cyril felt he had to say something. 'They say you kill for sport, Fergus.'

Fergus's thin lip curled. His yellow teeth showed in a smile of contempt. 'Humans kill us for sport. If I get into a hen coop the cackling goes to my head. I dispose of the lot. It's partly revenge. Do you know what that means, Cyril?'

Cyril said he wasn't sure.

'It means to pay back what you're owed — in blood. Humans are the most vengeful creatures under the sun. Once or twice every hundred years they kill each other for spite. History they call it. It's happening hereabouts every day. Up north they're as bad as you red and grey squirrels.'

'The humans I know,' Cyril said, 'live quietly.'

'Nothing is what it seems, Cyril.'

'Charlie told me. I know.'

'Do you?'

'I am up this tree because if I went down to talk it might be the end of my life.'

Fergus threw back his head and laughed silently, his eyes closed, but Cyril could see that he was being watched through two very narrow slits. Eventually, Fergus said, 'I don't eat squirrels.'

'I don't trust foxes,' Cyril said.

'You're quite a brat. You'll survive.'

'I hope to,' Cyril said.

As they were talking, Cyril noticed that two or three rabbits had come out of the ditch at the top of the Bracken Hill.

'Must take some exercise,' Fergus said, and loped off towards a big square stone about twenty yards from the ditch. The rabbits scurried away to their bunkers. For ten minutes Cyril watched Fergus get up on the stone, tumble off, and shake himself. Now and then he would lie on his back paddling his four feet in the air or keep very still as though sunning himself. Then he would shake himself, put his head on his paws and close his eyes. Though he was high and far away Cyril could see the narrow slits of Fergus's eyes and the gleam of watching. From the bunker entrances the rabbits watched these antics. Then, one by one they came out to nibble. Fergus continued tumbling from the stone, paddling the air, or lying dead still watching the rabbits through half-closed eyes. Cyril was fascinated. How strange other creatures were. Fergus was obviously up to something. Cyril was still wondering about this when he seemed, suddenly, to see double. He then understood. Fergus, in one pounce, had jumped from the stone and with a quick snap killed a rabbit. Then he went trotting off. It was all so sudden that Cyril could hardly believe it had happened. No wonder he was famed for cunning. Even as he had watched, Cyril had been so mesmerised that he could not imagine why Fergus kept repeating the same capers again and again. It would be a story for Charlie when he returned.

5

To Crom Castle

CYRIL COULD SEE from the sun that the day was advancing, so he decided to make his way quickly towards the river in search of Loughlin, the otter.

Firstly he had to get from the Bracken Hill to the river. That was simple. He went swinging down through the hedge, leapt across the road, and ran down the back of a ditch. In seconds he was up an oak tree at the river bank. The thing to do now was

study the landscape carefully, looking near and far to make sure there were no enemies crouching in wait. For five minutes he kept looking round and round. Most especially he studied the area on either side of the river. He could see nothing hostile. Below him there was a trout pool, and beyond it the water gurgled over stones — very different from the mirror stillness of the swans' lake.

Suddenly the water swirled and parted below him in the centre of the trout pool. Loughlin surfaced with a small, shining trout in her mouth. When Cyril whistled, she swam ashore immediately, swallowed the trout and gave a joyful cry. She clambered up the root of the tree. Lightly, happily, Cyril dropped to within a foot of his wet, whiskery, brown-eyed friend. Loughlin picked him up in her left paw and they rubbed noses, laughing, and Loughlin said, 'Someone told me you were dead.'

'I'm not.'

'I can see that.'

'My parents are.'

'Oh!'

'Yes.'

'How?'

'Gun.'

'When?'

'October last.'

'Ah! You poor little fellow. All alone?'

And so they talked for ten minutes about the long winter and the hard spring and how they had fared. Oscar, Loughlin's mate, had been caught in a net somewhere in Upper Lough Erne and drowned. She was so heartbroken she couldn't eat for days. When she began to hunt she was too weak to swim.

'December it was,' Loughlin said, 'and I very nearly died.'

'How did you manage?'

'Your neighbours, the swans, saw me crawling through a bog looking for something – anything – to eat. They told Charlie Badger. He came at once with food. I lived.'

'He never told me that.'

'Charlie's a saint.'

'Is he?'

'Well, maybe not quite, but good through and through.'

Cyril was amazed at this story. 'I thought swans didn't like you people'.

'They don't, but they're noble — they do the right thing even when they don't feel like it. It was a dark evening, snowing. I knew I was dying as I heard them fly overhead. They looked down but flew on. Then they sent Charlie. Life is full of strange things. But now you are alone too.'

'Very much.'

'Both of us now.' Loughlin brought Cyril closer to her great brown, liquid eyes and said, 'We should search together.'

'That's a good plan,' Cyril said. 'My very thought.'

Loughlin jumped into the pool, blew a mouthful of water into the air and shouted, 'Come on, Cyril, jump on my neck, and we'll swim to the river Finn, then to Crom Castle.'

Cyril was a little nervous. Did Loughlin really know what she was doing? She blew more water and dived under. When she was in the water it was impossible to talk to her.

Again she shouted, 'Come on, Cyril, jump.'

Without thinking, Cyril sprang from the bank onto Loughlin's neck, and suddenly the otter's powerful tail and paws thrust them down the tributary towards the Finn. Cyril had to hold on tightly. It was much, much faster than when he had been on Cynthia's back.

'Am I heavy on your neck?' Cyril asked.

'Can't feel you at all,' Loughlin said, and then asked, 'How will you manage if I go under?'

'I'm not sure,' Cyril said.

'Can you hold your breath?'

'I can try.'

'Then it should be all right,' Loughlin said.

Cyril had never been underwater in his life. He was nervous. 'Why go under?' he asked.

'Soon we'll be passing through lands full of cattle, and humans working at drains, through backyards and under bridges, and alongside roads. There may be danger. We may need to dive out of sight.'

Cyril could see that the river was leading directly towards a cottage with a small orchard and garden behind. There were piles of timber in a yard beside the river, and there was smoke coming from the cottage chimney. Beyond the cottage there was a small bridge.

'Will you dive under at that bridge?' Cyril asked.

'Depends,' Loughlin said.

'On what?'

'On what we see. What can you see, Cyril?'

'There's a man on a high hill walking through cattle.'

'He can't see us. What else?'

'Two cars are going over the bridge.'

'What else?'

'There's a woman coming out with a basket.'

'Yes?'

'She's hanging different shapes and colours in the air; they're flapping about.'

'Anything else?'

'There's a small human near the bridge.'

'Doing what?'

'Sitting with a stick.'

'A gun?'

'I can't see.'

'I'll have to dive — hold tight.'

Cyril grasped Loughlin's neck tightly and closed his eyes. It was not as cold as he expected. He was aware only that Loughlin had increased her speed. Cyril opened his eyes and stretched out his tail. It was murky, grey-green and brown all around, indistinct and dark, like the beech grove on a foggy winter's day, the light and shapes of trees and clouds glimmering strangely above.

We must be nearly at the bridge now, Cyril thought, when he felt a sudden sharp pain in the thumb of his left paw, then a wrench — and he was dangling in mid-air squeaking and wriggling with terror as pain darted from his thumb. He could see that a shiny hook was sticking into his flesh and realised that he was dangling from an ash rod. Holding the rod was a young male human staring at him with astonishment. He grabbed the line with his other paw and bit at the hook, trying to pull it out. The pain was so bad he screamed. Then he was swinging towards the bank. Immediately Cyril touched ground he felt safe. The boy was still holding the rod and staring when Cyril nipped the line and sprang towards the bridge. Because of the hook he had to run on three legs. He crossed the road and made straight for the shelter of high trees. From up there he watched the male human go to the house.

He watched two humans run out of the house followed by the black labrador dog that had chased him into the swans' lake. The dog barked loudly and then plunged into the river and began to swim upstream towards Loughlin. From his high perch Cyril saw the otter's shadow deep underwater as she swam away. When she came to a shallow, Loughlin was forced up and had to face the black dog. The dog barked, Loughlin bared her teeth and arched her back, then jumped backwards to where the water deepened. Then, suddenly, she was gone.

For quite a while the dog barked at the deep water. Cyril watched. Loughlin would by now be far away in some pool or lying in the safety of her holt near the river bank. He watched the humans talking to the boy. They were laughing. They did not believe his story about catching a squirrel. As Cyril looked at the hook in his thumb he was in no doubt about the story. His paw had begun to throb. Somehow he would have to get the hook out. But if he pulled at it now he knew he would cry out and perhaps be overheard by the humans. Painfully, he swung through the trees alongside the river, across the bridge at Knockballymore, dropped onto a garden wall and went on three legs towards a tumbledown summerhouse.

Crouching in a corner of the summerhouse he took the hook in his teeth and pulled it this way and that very gently. Pain twitched up his arm to his head. He stopped, looking at it. Somehow he would have to get it out. What a piece of bad luck. He tried again. The pain was so agonising that he squealed, but there was nothing for it but to go on pulling.

6

The Nightmare

CYRIL GRIPPED THE HOOK AGAIN and pulled as hard as he could. As the sharp jabbing pains went to his brain the white wings of unconsciousness closed his tormented eyes. Then Professor Maggers Jaggers, the great magpie surgeon, came sweeping in. He wore a white coat, white gloves and white wellies, and twelve magpie students in white stood reverently around. Professor Maggers Jaggers did not look into Cyril's face. He lifted the throbbing paw and said: 'Rotten. Incurable. I will talk now as I work, but no questions 'till I'm finished.'

A student magpie came forward with a grey paw on a steel tray and the Professor said: 'What we have here now is the left paw of a grey squirrel. I am going to remove the rotten member and attach this fresh grey one.'

Cyril kept his eyes tightly closed. A grey paw! He could hear Maggers Jaggers clacking brusquely to the silent students: 'This, of course, is a routine job. Sometime I hope to put a man's head on a dog's body, and a dog's head on a man's body. An amusing experiment, because most dogs are so stupid they worship humans and some humans so stupid they worship dogs! Of course, God has been experimenting for millions of years, but now we modern surgeons and scientists are overtaking God who has grown a little absentminded. Our motto must be "Onwards to the end", which like all true believers we trust will be a new beginning, and so on to everlasting.'

There was loud applause from the students. Professor Maggers Jaggers went off, striding down a steel corridor in his white wellies. Cyril lay quietly, aware that he was alone now. The throbbing had gone from his paw, but he was afraid to open his eyes and look. His left paw would be bigger, not his, with longer nails — and it would be grey! Even if it were perfect and gave him no pain, it made him feel sick to imagine it.

When he finally opened his eyes and looked, he saw that the hook was gone, the paw was his own and blood had congealed around the wound. It had all been a scary dream. He was so relieved he squeaked with delight: 'I'm alive, alive, alive! I am alive and well and care about nothing but to continue my quest for true love.' In the distance he could still see the bridge and the boy fishing by the river. He flexed his left paw; it felt fine. With a sudden shiver he realised that if the hook had caught in his throat, he would probably be dead by now. Life could end so suddenly. There was a day, an hour, a minute fixed somewhere in the great accounting book of death, his name marked: Cyril of Drumard. What a vast book that must be, Cyril thought. The thousands of millions of living things all had their moment of death. The day had begun with the old crow's death, and here he was still thinking about death. It is not good to be so gloomy, he thought. Also, he was hungry. From the garden wall he could see beautiful apples hanging in red clusters, tree after tree after tree. His mouth watered. He looked back carefully at the old high house with the red door, at the fields beyond and terraced lawns leading down to a lake. He looked towards Drumard and saw the crown of beech trees where he lived. Slowly he realised that he was in the garden at Knockballymore, and as he stared his heart missed a beat. Chilling thoughts came — an orchard, a terraced lawn, a long lake. Yes, this was the garden where both his parents had been shot dead last autumn. His body became suddenly paralysed. Was there a human, hidden somewhere with a gun, watching? Sitting in the old summerhouse he realised why rabbits go rigid with terror.

I'm not a rabbit, he said to himself, I'm a squirrel and squirrels are courageous. I must not be stupid, he thought. There was neither sight nor sound nor scent of danger, only the horror of knowing what had happened in this place. How awful that a place so quiet, fruitful and beautiful should also be a place of blood and death.

He crept along the roof of the summerhouse towards the rafters of a derelict glasshouse, his ears pricked for danger,

then jumped from that to an apple tree, and from this to the safety of a high beech. So this was the place. What instinct had brought him here? On the very day of his quest for true love he had found the orchard of death.

Was there a hidden meaning in this? Did it mean that if he continued his quest, if he journeyed on towards Crom Castle, he himself would meet death? Or was it nature's way of saying, You must take care. Who had told him to take care? He tried to remember. The swans? Fergus Fox? Charlie?

'I must go back to Charlie,' he said aloud. Slowly, sitting a hundred feet above the orchard, his courage returned.

When his courage was fully restored he set out again, leaping and soaring through the townlands of Lisnaroe and Killrooskey, 'till he was back at Drumard and the bog road where Charlie lived. Without his usual polite squeak of warning, he darted into the main chamber. Mrs B. pointed at three badger cubs asleep on the dry rushes. Cyril nodded. He would be quiet. Charlie seemed slightly startled. He had his far-away thinker's face on.

'Cyril!' he said. 'How extraordinary. You look exhausted.'

'Shush,' Mrs B. said.

Charlie pointed to a tunnel that led off the main chamber. This second chamber was lit from a pothole in the road above. It was pleasant enough and the rushes smelled fresh and clean.

Mrs B. said, 'You should always knock or give some warning sign.'

'I'm sorry,' Cyril said.

'Always,' she repeated.

'Yes,' Cyril said.

'There's no room in this sett for privacy, and I'll tell you how old fashioned it is — two hundred years, that's how long it's been lived in. It's time to move, but Charlie won't. He's useless. I've been trying to convince him for years. Life can be very trying.'

For a while there was quite a silence.

'I think,' Charlie said, 'we are boring Cyril now.'

'No, no,' Cyril said.

'Of course we are,' Charlie said. 'You came darting in here, your eyes bulging with fright, out of breath and clearly over-wrought, and straight off we start talking of . . .' he paused and looked at his mate, then said quietly, 'other things. Tell us, has your quest for true love gone awry? Have you stumbled on misfortune? Or have you merely been hounded like the rest of us?'

'Well,' Cyril said, 'yes — and no.'

'Take your time, Cyril, compose yourself and tell us all.'

So Cyril began and told all that had befallen him on his journey north. Half-way through his tale he noticed that Mrs B. was listening with great attention. When he came to the part about how Charlie had helped Loughlin to survive, Mrs B. interrupted. 'Did you do that, Charles? You never told me.'

'She'd do the same for me,' Charlie growled.

'I think it was a wonderful and courageous thing to do.'

'I agree,' Cyril said, and went on with his story — the hook, the hospital dream, the sudden terrifying realisation of being in the orchard where his parents had been shot, a sense of overwhelming loss and loneliness. All this, he said, had driven him back to the bog road and his dear friends, the badgers. Mrs B. had tears in her eyes.

'And I was shushing you and talking about our troubles.'

She picked Cyril up. 'Do please forgive me, Cyril. Show me your paw.'

Cyril put out his left paw. There was congealed blood near the wrist. Very gently Mrs B. put her nose close to the wound. 'Clean,' she said, 'and healing. You are a strange little parcel of fortune and misfortune.'

'I know,' Cyril said.

'And I do think, Charles, that sending such a little mite on such a quest was dangerous. He could be dead.'

Charlie shook his head. 'Loneliness, my love, is worse than death. He must continue the quest. It is not normal for a squirrel to be lonely.'

'This is true,' Cyril said.

Charlie put up his right paw. He always did that when he was about to make a wise pronouncement. 'One thing occurs to me about your dream at midday — does anything strike you, Cyril?'

Cyril put a claw between his teeth and thought. He hadn't a notion what Charlie was getting at.

'The new paw in your dream,' Charlie said, 'was grey, not red.'

Cyril shrugged.

'You mustn't shrug. It is very important. Your dream shows that in your heart of hearts, you want to be at peace with your grey cousins. Love creates, hatred destroys.'

'What can I do?' Cyril said. 'Every grey I meet tries to bite or injure me in some way.'

Charlie looked up at the pot-hole for quite a while as he considered his reply. 'I'll be honest. I don't know how you can make peace. I know only that hatred destroys.'

Somewhere in the big chamber the badger cubs began to whimper. 'I must go to my little ones,' Mrs B. said. 'But now that I know what you're seeking, I'll be in fear and dread until I hear you're safe. Do take the utmost care. We both love you.'

'I'll be fine,' Cyril said.

'We must plan your next move,' Charlie said. 'You've tried going west. Where did "our friends" say the other squirrel family lived?'

'At Annamakerrig, east of here. Old Falvey and his three daughters. But I don't think I would make it. It would be very dangerous.'

'You must try to get there — but this time more safely. Let's go outside and ponder.'

7

East to Annamakerrig

OUTSIDE IT WAS SUNNY, and the yellow claw-like leaves of the sycamore were spinning down from the tree above and lying about on the ground. Suddenly, Cyril saw a familiar head a few fields away. It was Bercan, the hare, sitting up as hares do on his hind quarters surveying the surrounding fields, hills, lake and landscape.

Charlie was shortsighted and could not see far, so Cyril said: 'I can see Bercan on a ditch in Tiernahinch. Will I whistle to him? Would he take me east?'

Charlie said, 'Do', then lowered his voice as Bercan approached, and warned Cyril: 'If he agrees to take you to Annamakerrig, be careful. At times he can be giddy, foolish or aggressive, or all those things at once.'

'I don't understand his jokes,' Cyril said, 'or when he puts a "B" in front of every word.'

'His B language! That is silliness,' Charlie said, 'and doesn't matter. But when he gets up on a tree stump and shouts "Death to humans" or "Blind their dogs" and such things, it does matter and could be dangerous for himself.'

'I've never seen him like that,' Cyril said.

Charlie cleared his throat. 'My grandfather,' he said, 'was a wise old brock and he used to say about hares that "there's just a wee want." But, like most excitable creatures, he can be very sane in calmer moments — but do take care.'

Bercan came bounding over, leaping sideways over clumps of rushes, making a comic pattern. As he arrived at Charlie's sett he tumbled three times, ending on his hind quarters and clapping his two front paws. Cyril was delighted with the performance and squeaked in welcome.

'Ho, ho, Mr Cyril, you beech rogue. How are you anyway?' shouted Bercan, in greeting.

'I'm well, almost every way,' Cyril said.

'Good boy, Charlie,' Bercan said, winking and grinning at Charlie. He gave a few further shouts and winks, and muttered B language under his breath — a trick he had of putting a 'B' in front of every word so that he could say things and confuse people at the same time! He delighted in confusion. Charlie found it all very tiresome.

Suddenly, Bercan shouted to nobody in particular, 'What do cowslips remind you of?'

'I give up,' Cyril said. Charlie looked away and said nothing.

'Bull trunks, you dimwits!'

Cyril laughed more at Bercan's screaming at his own joke than at the joke itself, until Charlie interrupted, told Bercan about Cyril's quest and explained slowly what had happened to Cyril that morning. Bercan listened, his ears gradually drooping, his eyes bulging more and more as Charlie told the story.

Finally, he said: 'Poor Cyril. That is scarifying for such a small beech nut. You must learn to look about you. Use your eyes back and front like me.'

'But I do feel his quest should continue,' said Charlie, 'don't you?'

'The quest for true love is a noble one,' agreed Bercan.

'"Our friends",' Charlie said, nodding his head towards the hump...

'Bousy, baxing bats!' Bercan shouted suddenly in B language, meaning, of course, lousy, taxing rats!

'Yes,' Charlie said evenly, '"our friends" are certain there is a red squirrel family in the forest district of Annamakerrig. Do you know Annamakerrig, Bercan?'

'Bintimately.'

'I would think,' Charlie said, 'it's about a hundred fields or so from here. Am I right?'

'Bright!' Bercan screamed.

'Would you consider taking Cyril there? He's such a small fellow, but nothing in this land can catch you.'

As Bercan inflated his chest at this praise, Cyril realised that Charlie was a shrewd old flatterer. Bercan suddenly winked again and asked, 'What's the cure for a hare who's had too much?'

Too much of what? Cyril wondered. Then he caught Charlie's eye.

'A good plunge in a deep river,' answered Charlie.

'Wrong!' screamed Bercan. 'A hair of the dog that bit it.'

He giggled at this, then burst out laughing until Charlie said, without a trace of a smile: 'An excellent riddle' — then, 'Can you make it to Annamakerrig, Bercan?'

'A matter of honour,' Bercan said, then winked at Cyril and ordered, 'Jump up, Cyril.'

Cyril jumped up as he was told and before he had time to say goodbye to Charlie, Bercan shouted, 'Farewell, Charlie. Be of good cheer.'

8

Along the old Railway Line

HOLDING BERCAN'S NECK with a paw, Cyril lifted his other paw towards Charlie, who smiled, raising both paws in solemn and loving farewell. How extraordinary it was to be astride Bercan's flexing shoulders; the sense of power and speed was very exciting even for a squirrel. In less than a minute the crown of beech trees was out of sight and they were well under way, this time travelling east. Almost within minutes, it seemed, they were within sight of Clones with its two hills, two churches, round tower and Celtic cross, Bercan taking huge leaps when they came to ditches and bogs, or making strange sudden patterns in open fields when alerted by odd scents or sounds.

He paused at the new graveyard at the townland of Clonkeencole, ran down the parish priest's avenue, past the old people's home, cut into bottom lands by the side of a small stream 'till they came to the derelict railway beyond Bishopscourt.

Bercan paused and said, 'That was a dodgy bit,' and before Cyril could reply they were off again, loping easily along the railway line, sometimes high above the countryside, often in the deep ravine of an embankment 'till suddenly they came upon a great bog with massive pillars rising out of it. The railway seemed to come to an end. Follow the railway line, King Rat had said, Cyril remembered.

'Where's it gone?' Cyril asked.

'There used to be a steel bridge over that — a viaduct,' and Bercan pointed to where the railway line began again half a mile away.

Bercan went down into the bog and made straight for one of the stone pillars. He paused near it, watching a small footbridge that crossed the river —listening, smelling, looking. All seemed clear. He crossed the bridge and went straight up the high embankment. They were now over a hundred feet above the river in the townland of Ballinure. 'That's the second part,' Bercan said.

'Don't you want to stop?' Cyril asked.

Bercan's ears dropped back. 'No, no, not here.'

'It seems safe,' said Cyril.

'Safe from living things,' Bercan said, and his ears drooped back even more as he stared up the railway line towards a small overtrack bridge. 'Humans were digging here a hundred years ago,' he said. 'Then it fell in and they died, a lot of them. I was passing one night,' he dropped his voice, 'strange cries, moanings, weepings, howls.' He paused as the memory returned and Cyril could hear muttered B talk, and just make out things like 'bodeful bridge, black birchen birds, blind bug-a-boos' and 'bidnight'. Bercan shook his head strangely. 'I was

caught once by living humans. I got away. I won't be caught by dead ones.'

Cyril felt his blood begin to chill. 'Could they catch you, the dead ones?'

Bercan said, 'Who knows?' and added, 'Maybe not. But I don't like this place.'

Away below they could see the farms laid out on either side of the river, and the farm lanes and the country roads. Far away on a sloping drumlin they could see a forage harvester chopping fresh grass into a silage wagon. Only a small triangle of the field remained. Bercan was watching very intently as the machine moved closer to the last swathe. Cyril could see that he was growing more and more agitated. As the great machine was bearing down on the last few yards a young hare leapt from the lush grass and with a sudden burst of speed was out of the field and gone from sight. Bercan came down off his back legs and took a deep breath. He was blinking very rapidly.

'How did you know?' Cyril asked.

'There's always some young fool of a hare in the last swathe.' He paused and muttered, 'Barvest, a berrifying business.' He beat his paws against his chest making a strange drumming sound and then suddenly spoke in a loud voice so that Cyril could hear above the drumming noise. 'Worse ... long ago ...'

'What was worse?' Cyril asked.

'Harvesting,' Bercan said, 'because in those days when it came to the last swathe the humans came at us with sticks and shouts of *"cailleach, cailleach"* — "witches, witches". We hares were thought to be witches and were killed in hundreds long ago, in every field all over this land. And when they're not killing us in cornfields they're chasing us with big hounds or trapping and netting us for sport with greyhounds, all because of LIES,' he shouted.

A sudden small wind flurried the water far below. 'No one traps the wind,' Bercan said hoarsely, 'or hunts it with greyhounds, or lies about it. But they tell lies about me, about us hares. And why? Because we do a love dance in spring? Because we leap for joy? Because we beat our chests? Because we tumble?' He paused suddenly, trembling, and turned to Cyril. 'Do you think I am mad?'

'No, no,' Cyril said.

Gradually, Bercan's trembling eased. Cyril found himself looking at the hare, wondering was he a little mad. Which was the real Bercan — the creature who laughed and tumbled and told silly jokes or the trembling creature brooding about hunting and humans and madness? Suddenly, Bercan screwed up his eyes at the sun and said: 'The day's near spent, my wee boyo, and your quest is still a question mark and I have a riddle to make up before dark. Hop up. We'll travel through a few townlands, go round a lake and then we'll be in the great forest of Annamakerrig.

Soon they were away, down through the stubble of a long sloping field at Latroe. They went on past the village of Lisdarragh, keeping all the while to the old railway till they came to the townland of Drumgristin where Bercan turned sharply down off the railway track, made straight for Feagh Lough, skirted round it loping on 'till they reached the top of a high hill at Crappagh. There he stopped suddenly and pointed ahead with both short front feet.

'There,' he said, 'Borest bof Bannamakerrig!'

9

The Forest of Annamakerrig

CYRIL'S HEART LEAPT with excitement. About half a mile away he could see a magnificent stretch of forest country, a lake far longer than any of the lakes in the ten townlands, an old house surrounded by hardwood trees and an orchard all yellow, gold and brown in the late September sun.

Before he had time to say anything, Bercan was away again. Soon they were deep in the forest. Twice Bercan sniffed the ground and changed direction, then suddenly, in a small alder glade, lying close together, they came upon fallow deer — six does and two bucks. They were cudding quietly and looked mildly surprised as Bercan approached. Cyril thought that Bercan might confuse them so he decided to tell his own story. He dropped from Bercan's neck and, sweeping his tail over his head by way of greeting those gracious creatures, he told his tale, looking into their brown inquiring eyes.

They all stopped cudding. They seemed to listen with attention and sympathy, muttering now and then: 'Poor little mite. God help him. What a tiny morsel. How he's suffered.'

Eventually it was the old buck who spoke: 'There's only one red squirrel in this forest — old Falvey, and he paired with a grey.'

Cyril listened, shocked. He felt his heart grown leaden. 'A grey!' he squeaked. 'Impossible.'

'It's true,' the buck said, 'and he has three beautiful daughters.'

For ten seconds Cyril was so stunned he said nothing. Then he asked, cautiously, 'What colour are the daughters, red or grey?'

'Neither,' the buck said.

Then all the does began speaking at once: 'They're all different.'

'One's red as a midsummer sun.'

'One's silver like a winter moon.'

'The third's like a field of autumn barley.'

'They are called Roisin, Triona and Una.'

'Let's go to Falvey,' the buck said, and they all moved off together, bucks and does walking in stately single line, Cyril above them in the pine trees, Bercan, impatient at the leisurely pace, running in circles and letting out odd shouts and yahoos.

When they arrived at an oak tree near a boathouse the old buck nodded upwards. Cyril saw the small drey of a red squirrel in the fork of a mighty branch. His heart was pulsing rapidly as he ran up and squeaked a greeting. Would one of the three daughters appear? Abruptly, a head poked through the opening. It was Falvey himself, all bushy eyebrows over eyes that looked at once wise and wicked. His whiskers were white.

'Who are you?' his voice was deep and most un-squirrel-like.

Cyril explained, feeling so shy that his voice dropped almost to a whisper. Falvey looked away. There was a silence, and then he said, 'My three girls are asleep in their drey.'

Again there was quite a silence and Falvey looked so cross that Cyril did not know what to expect. Suddenly Falvey was out of the drey and said, 'Let's go and see.'

Not far away there was a huge pine tree that looked hundreds of years old. Half way up this there was an opening. Cyril crept up and looked in shyly, blinking with wonder. The drey was large and round inside and lined with soft grass and downy feathers, mostly blue and green. Asleep on the floor of the nest were Falvey's three daughters. As Cyril looked from one to the other, it seemed to him that they were all equally delicate and beautiful. His eyes stayed longest on the one most like a red squirrel in colour. Falvey was sitting on a branch ten feet down.

'Wake them and see what happens,' Falvey suggested. 'I'll be in my drey.'

And Falvey left as abruptly as he had appeared. Cyril felt very timid and confused. If there were only one maybe he could manage, or even two, but three! What would Charlie do in such a case? He tried to think but couldn't. He would have to do what Falvey suggested — wake them up and see what happened. He crept into the drey and sat watching them, his heart racing — the blonde, the silver, and the light copper. He gave a very low whistle. They wakened, blinking and staring at him with surprise and curiosity. It was the silver one who smiled and spoke first. 'Who are you?'

Cyril's voice went very odd as he told them his name. He did not dare say he was looking for true love.

Eventually the copper one said, 'You're Cyril, you're here, so what?'

'My quest,' Cyril said, avoiding their eyes, 'is for true love.'
They all burst out laughing.

Eventually it was the silver one who intervened, her voice very soft: 'You must think us all very rude. My name is Triona and this is Una,' pointing at the blonde squirrel, 'and, of course, Roisin,' pointing to the copper.

Roisin immediately said, with a shrug, 'Count me out — I don't want a mate or a nest of little squeakers, and I think true love is a silly notion,' and she left before Cyril had time to reply.

'Does she mean that?' Cyril asked the other two.

'It's what she always says,' Triona said.

In the silence that followed both girl squirrels kept looking elsewhere. Cyril was nervous but at least now there were only two to be afraid of instead of three. Triona and Una, silver and blonde. Eventually, Triona asked, 'Are you hungry?'

Cyril wasn't hungry, but he hesitated, and she said immediately: 'A few fresh acorns? I'll get some.'

'Thank you,' Cyril said. As she swept past him the swish of her tail and the scent of her body made his head go light.

When she had gone the blonde one came over very close to him and said, 'Do you snore?'

'Snore?' Cyril asked. 'I don't know. How could I know?'

'Triona does. And she steals and is very lazy.'

Cyril was dismayed. A stealing, snoring, lazy mate was not what he was questing, but when Triona returned with a handful of acorns he found it hard to believe that she was as her sister had described her. Also, he noticed as they talked that Triona was quick and generous in praise of her sisters, but the blonde one kept looking into his eyes and said nothing in praise of either sister. As he was about to leave, he was astonished when the blonde one came over, took his head between her paws and nuzzled him affectionately. He felt awkward and darted out.

For an hour he sat on a branch watching the lake and thinking. Truly, all he wanted was to gather nuts, re-line his old drey, have a few more talks with Charlie, then go to sleep for the winter. True love was all too confusing and dangerous — and yet, and yet, the winter was long and lonely and dark and full of strange dreams. Life is but a little thing — you grow old, your strength goes, and then there's nothing you can do but cry for what might have been. Better to take a risk.

When Cyril had left the nest Roisin returned and asked, 'Has the great lover gone?'

Una pointed out to where Cyril was sitting three trees away, staring into the depths of the forest.

'What's he thinking?' Roisin asked.

'What are we thinking?' asked Triona.

Roisin looked first at Una, then at Triona. 'I think he's silly.

This questing — all that true love stuff. He's so old fashioned. And the nervous blinking and twitching, it's a bit off. It makes me more certain than ever I don't want to pair — with anyone. Certainly he's not for me.'

'Nor me,' Una said.

'How can you be so certain?' Triona asked.

'I'm sure he's as good as all the rest of them but he's not for me.'

There was quite a silence until Triona asked, 'Why not?'

Una said: 'I'd prefer a squirrel with a limp, or a squint, or some half-mad obsession. A slight defect. He's all health and vigour. There's something too ordinary about him. I think he's a bit of a simpleton.'

There was quite a pause, then both sisters looked at Triona. 'What do you think, Triona?'

'I think,' she said, 'he's perfect. Just beautiful.'

For the next half hour both Una and Roisin tried to unsay what they had said, until Triona stated: 'I don't mind what you think. I know what I feel.'

Cyril could hear the squirrels talking in the nest. I must have courage, he said to himself, and swung back to the great pine. As he approached, Roisin and Una came out and sprang away out of sight.

Triona came to the entrance. She seemed very shy, but kept looking steadily into his eyes as she asked him questions about his life. What was it like where he lived? He answered, feeling that he was talking too much, but he did not know how to stop. There was so much to describe. The great green cliffs of beech. The abundance of beech nuts. The bluebells and wild garlic below. The raspberry field. The orchard, full of apples and plums. And on fine days you could count maybe thirty drumlin lakes, and see the cathedral spires of Monaghan and Armagh. You could watch the swallows coming and going, see the great aeroplanes flying around the world. You could watch the huntsmen hunting and see Bercan and Fergus outwitting the hounds. You could watch the cattle and sheep and the farmers farming. It was never dull, he said, and no matter what the weather it was always beautiful. He paused and asked, 'Does that sound all right?' When Triona nodded, Cyril spun away and within seconds was back at Falvey's nest.

The old squirrel came out, his piercing eyes full of inquiry.

'Roisin,' Cyril said at once, 'says she'll never mate, and thinks love is silly.'

'She is a modern creature,' Falvey said, 'unsuited to a simple squirrel like yourself.'

Cyril did not like being told he was simple, but ignored the comment. 'Una tells me Triona is greedy, snores at night and is lazy.'

Falvey looked away for about half a minute before asking, 'Do you believe what Una says?'

'I don't know what to believe,' Cyril said.

Falvey shouted suddenly: 'Do you believe what she says, yes or no? Answer me.'

After a pause, Cyril said firmly, 'No.'

'You're right,' Falvey said. 'Una was speaking of herself more than her sister. Sometimes we accuse others of faults that lie in ourselves.'

'Then, Sir,' Cyril said, 'may I pair with your daughter, Triona?'

'Don't ask me, ask her,' said Falvey.

Cyril raced back and ran up the great pine. The nest was empty but Triona was sitting out on a long branch below. She was looking at humans water-skiing on the lake below. Cyril dropped down beside her and watched too. When the speedboat was out of sight, he ventured quietly, 'I was hoping...'

'I was hoping...' he tried again, looking for the right words. He paused. Triona looked at him and said, 'So was I.'

'Is that yes?' he asked.

'Yes,' she said.

In seconds, Cyril was back with old Falvey, who, before Cyril could speak, growled, 'When?'

'Tonight, by moonlight.' Cyril said.

'Where?'

'The beechwood at Drumard.'

Falvey stared severely, then spoke so quickly and angrily that Cyril could scarcely follow: 'I don't know you. Who are you? An idler? A worker? What's your larder like? Have you made provision for the winter, the coldest ever on its way? What is your land area, your gathering talent? How many nests do you have? Who are your friends, your enemies? I know you are a bounder — all squirrels are natural bounders — but what sort of bounder? Look at that person down there,' Falvey said pointing down at Bercan. 'You came here with that idiot. Are you his friend?'

Cyril was so shaken by the suddenness of this outburst that he looked down obediently and saw Bercan sitting upright on his hind legs, smiling foolishly. 'Yes,' he said, loyally.

'He's insane. If your friends are insane, it follows that you yourself must be somewhat unsound. How dare you presume to take my silver daughter to some wretched scrub I've never heard of.'

It seemed to Cyril that Falvey was as mad in his own way as Bercan but, of course, he could not say that. 'What can I do?' Cyril asked, quietly.

'I want proof, evidence, that you are sound in mind and body.'

'How can I prove that?' Cyril asked.

'Whom do you know?'

Cyril listed off the various friends and acquaintances who might speak warmly for him, and was wondering how he would convince Falvey when he heard a familiar sound. Looking down he saw the swans gliding towards the lake, their black-webbed feet outstretched, their great wings reflecting in the still water. They landed, ruffling their feathers, paddling and looking about. What a bit of good fortune. 'Would they do?' Cyril asked, pointing.

Cyril could see at once that Falvey was impressed. He pretended not to be. 'Do they know you?'

'Yes.'

'How well?'

'Well enough.'

Falvey was off immediately. In a minute he was atop an alder tree at the lake's edge signalling to the swans. Cyril watched them float over. They talked for five minutes. Every now and then Cyril could see Cedric and Cynthia nodding and shaking their heads. Then Falvey came sprinting back, and said almost angrily, 'They seem to think you're foolish, but decent.' He held his paw towards Cyril, who took it. When Bercan saw the two red squirrels with paws joined he tumbled and cheered loudly three times: 'Bhree bheers burray! Bhree bheers burray! Bhree bheers burray!'

'What's that half-wit howling about?' Falvey asked.

'Just being cheerful,' Cyril said.

'Now, about the pairing,' Falvey said. 'This wood you inhabit, tell me about it.'

'About a hundred beech trees,' Cyril said, 'some of them two hundred years old.'

'That's not a wood,' Falvey growled, 'it's a shelter belt. The pairing will have to take place here in our forest. I'll make all the provisions. Whom do you want here?'

'All my friends and neighbours,' Cyril said.

'All!' Falvey growled.

'All who want to come.'

Falvey thought for a moment, then said, 'Very well,' and sprang away.

10

The Pairing Party

CYRIL DROPPED TO THE GROUND, called Bercan and explained to him about the pairing and how he would like Charlie and Mrs B., the foxes, or indeed any neighbour creatures who wanted to come. He asked Bercan would he be able to contact and invite them.

'Pairing party!' yelled Bercan, delighted.

'Yes,' Cyril said, shyly.

'Bexcellent! Boyful! Bonderful!' Bercan shouted.

'What about "our friends" the rats?' Cyril asked.

Bercan shook his head and said: 'I hate rats. Bousy, baxing bats. Never!'

Cyril suggested that the pairing between a half-grey and the only red squirrel for miles around was perhaps a special affair. In festive company King Rat might even be persuaded to tax less harshly. Bercan thought about this, and then muttered: 'Maybe. Very well so. I must go.'

'Yes,' Cyril said, 'bime is bcarce,' falling into B language to please Bercan.

Bercan gave another whoop of joy and went cantering west. Cyril raced through the pine branches down to the lake to invite the swans to the pairing. They accepted, graciously.

'Congratulations,' Cedric said. 'How considerate and charming.'

'A moonlight marriage,' Cynthia smiled, 'what a pleasing and pleasant prospect.'

'Can we contact our close connections?' Cedric asked. 'Crows, daws, magpies, pheasants, crakes, grouse, woodcock, snipe, larks, blackbirds, thrushes, robins, curlews, sparrows, owls, and even hawks? We'll see they all behave well,' Cedric said.

'Why not?' Cyril replied.

And the swans flew off into the evening sun. As Cyril watched them go he felt suddenly exhausted. It had been a long, tense and very exciting day. In a few hours' time he would be paired. He would have to be fresh. He curled his tail around his head and fell asleep. He woke when he heard his name being called. It was night and the moon was high over the lake. Below him he could hear the cudding of does. When he looked down, the forest was alive with creatures, so many and mixed, that for a moment he found it difficult to make out who was who.

Charlie was there with Mrs B. who was wearing a strange hat made with rushes, with a feather sticking out of it. She was talking to Vivienne Fox, who was wearing glamorous earrings. Fergus was listening to Charlie with a little smile. They were drinking amber liquid out of hollow turnips. Loughlin was there too, her otter's tail wagging as she listened to Bercan who could not be heard above the clamour of the squeaking, friendly growling, the twittering and chirping of bird noise.

Professor Maggers Jaggers was there in a very smart swallow-tailed suit, surrounded by hundreds of birds who were listening to him with their mouths wide open.

It was only then that Cyril realised that there were as many birds as animals, some on the ground, more in branches. There were hundreds of rabbits hopping about, all too busy eating to talk to anyone. Most astonishing of all, two dozen grey squirrels were scurrying about with half-acorns and turnips full of the amber liquid. Falvey, Roisin and Una were dispensing from a spring well that seemed full of fermenting nuts. Cyril rubbed his eyes. Where was his mate, Triona? As he wondered, a soft voice came from the branch above, 'I didn't want to waken you.' She was sitting on the branch just above him, a necklace of tiny green acorns about her silver throat, her eyes shining.

Suddenly, a silence fell on the whole gathering. They all looked towards the lake. A large plank came floating towards the shore. From this plank King Rat jumped, and after him about two hundred rats. They came, scuttling and hissing, towards the centre of the clearing. His eyes bright, King Rat stood on his hind legs and looked around. He was wearing a very finely woven cloak of chicken bones, clasped at the neck by the skull of some small creature. Falvey sprang from the well with an acorn of the liquid and said, 'You are most welcome, Sire.'

King Rat took the acorn in his claw and handed it to a guard rat who tasted it and nodded. The King then took it back. His mouth was smiling but his eyes were cold as he said, 'We rats are honoured to be invited here, and deeply impressed by this gathering from so many fields, lakes, trees and drumlins.'

There was a low murmur and restrained applause.

'Where is our little red neighbour and his spouse to be?' the King asked.

Falvey sprang to the bottom of the tree and pointed upwards towards Cyril and Triona who were now sitting together on a branch. Triona had tied white berries around Cyril's throat. Suddenly there was a tumultuous clapping and a great flapping of wings, mixed in with barks, howling and screeching, and cheers of goodwill. As the applause lessened Cyril saw the swans high above the lake, circling round and round, gliding

lower until they came directly to the point where the pairing was to take place. They splashed into the water and came ashore, walking very slowly to avoid any impression of waddling as they approached. Cynthia was wearing a simple cloak of water lily leaves and Cedric had a water lily pinned to his chest.

They approached with a mat of sedge and laid it in the centre of the clearing. Falvey then led the way down and they stood on this mat, Cyril on one side and Triona on the other. Falvey waited for silence, then took both tails, the glossy silver and the deep copper red, and joined both above his head. The applause was so overwhelming that Cyril felt tears coming into his eyes.

Eventually, Falvey raised a paw for silence. 'I wish to speak on this occasion. Years ago I was paired in secret because of the hatred between the reds and the greys. Sadly, that feeling persists. We are all creatures, living as best we can. We share the same water, the same fields and ditches and boglands, the same sky, the same seasons, the same joys and sorrows, and the same long sleep that ends it all. Certain things occur from time to time which I shall not mention tonight, but nothing to match the horror of what humans do to each other, and to us, and to the world we inhabit.'

This statement was greeted with loud applause, and Falvey went on: 'Tonight, because of Triona and Cyril, there is a feeling of goodwill. We must hope that this will continue.'

As the applause faded after Falvey's speech, Cyril realised that everyone was looking at him, and that he was expected to say something. The presence of all the animals and birds confused him, and he could think of nothing to say, so he managed to stutter, 'I am very happy.'

They all waited for Cyril to continue, but he could think of nothing else, so, in one leap he made three somersaults which delighted the great assemblage of birds and beasts. When the noise began to ease, King Rat stepped onto the matting, very erect on his hind legs, his cloak of bones clinking. Around him in widening circles were his huge, crouching body-guards, all with their teeth bared and their fixed smiles. Under his cloak the sleekness of his body shone greyly in the light of the moon. He jerked his head this way and that until there was total silence.

'We are all delighted,' he said, 'for our little neighbour, Cyril. Falvey of Annamakerrig has spoken well. He talks of peace and goodwill, and blames humans for most of the horrors we must endure — and rightly so. Naturally, as close cousins of the grey squirrel family we are delighted at this pairing. To mark this happy midnight, all taxes imposed will be dropped.'

The applause was thunderous. When it had faded, King Rat looked around, his cold eyes glittering like diamonds as he smiled and said, 'For a while, at least.'

Here and there, there was some snarling and hissing and Cedric was heard to say in a loud voice, 'Wretched rat.' In the midst of this hubbub, Fergus Fox came forward and said he was responsible for the breaking of at least one human neck and many human bones in hunting. Bercan greeted this with a hysterical cheer. Fergus grinned at him, waited for silence and for another ten minutes he boasted about how clever he was and what a cunning enemy of humans, and how he destroyed all their tame geese, ducks and hens. In the end he remembered he was at a pairing, and he turned to Cyril and Triona and wished them well.

'A disorderly, disgusting discourse,' Cedric said.

Loughlin and Bercan began speaking together. One was so confused and the other so excited that nobody understood either, and for that reason their speeches were warmly received until Bercan, who seemed disgruntled, got up again, this time on a tree stump where the whole assembly could see him. His eyes were pulsing strangely, his ears flat against his neck. As he spoke his voice seemed slurred but there was no mistaking what he said when he shouted:

'Cage the hunter humans — loose them one by one to a pack of mad dogs — let them be ripped to pieces — let them squeal with terror and let them die, thus, as we do...' he paused, trembling. He didn't seem to know where he was or what he had said. In the odd hush that followed, Charlie ambled over, put a paw on Bercan's shoulders and whispered something. Cedric turned to Cynthia and said quietly, 'Incoherent and insane. This has limped on too long.' He held up a wing, saying that he felt things had got out of hand a little and that he and Cynthia would be happy to fly the happy pair back to the wood at Drumard.

The eating and drinking had been continuous throughout the evening. The troupe of grey squirrels were energetic about keeping everyone supplied. Huge hoards of nuts and herbs and piles of berries along with the well of fermented acorns and crushed elderberries had been well depleted. Finally, Falvey requested silence and said: 'There is a wise thinker among us who has not spoken. We'll give him the last word.'

Everyone looked at Charlie as silence fell. Looking rather abashed he said: 'As a close friend of Cyril's I can only say my heart is full. It has been said of me that I am a sad badger. Tonight I am a glad badger. Cyril's quest is over. The journey is completed. He has said he is happy. So am I.' He paused for a moment to engage Bercan's attention, then stretched his arms to include the whole crowd and said, 'I give you Cyril and Triona — a toast to the future, to true love and to peace.'

In the hullabaloo that followed Charlie's closing toast, Cedric craned his neck towards Charlie and said, 'A most moving memory.'

Triona kissed Falvey and her two sisters and walked with Cyril towards the lake. Alongside them hundreds of animals ran barking, bleating messages of goodwill. Above them in the air was the drumming of thousands of birds, singing and chirping with joy.

At the lake Cedric and Cynthia walked into the shallow water, their wings arched and waiting. Together Cyril and Triona leapt from the shore, landing neatly on the swans.

Almost, it seemed, in slow motion the swans moved forward towards the middle of the lake. Then their great wings began to beat majestically, churning the still waters of the great lake into a myriad of drowning stars. They took off and in a minute the lake was gone, and they were high in the silent sky over the dark pattern of fields, high over townlands and villages, familiar to Cyril because of his journey with Bercan. When he was not looking down he glanced over at Triona and it seemed to Cyril that nothing he had ever seen was more beautiful than a silver squirrel, her eyes lit up in the moon, sitting astride Cynthia's white back. When they came to the beech wood of Drumard the swans circled three times, coming closer and closer until finally they were gliding low and slow over the branches of the high beech. As they approached, Cyril said to Triona, 'Now.'

And both dropped onto the branches. The swans went on gliding over the wood down to their own lake, the lake of Burdantien, which means the lake of burning light. For a long time both squirrels looked out at the surrounding countryside. Soon it would be October, days growing dark and cold, lakes and rivers brimming, swallows gone, the rest of the leaves tired like old people who have worked all their days and want only sleep and peace in the quiet earth. Year's end. For Cyril the quest for true love was over. For both of them life was just beginning.

The Animals in Real Life

BY NATURALIST OSCAR MERNE

The Red and Grey Squirrel

Sciurus vulgaris (red)   *Iora Rua*

Sciurus carolinensis (grey)   *Iora Glas*

Squirrels are rodents, members of the order *Rodentia*, and therefore related to rats and mice. In Ireland there are two species – the native red squirrel, and the introduced North American grey squirrel which has been here since 1911. Grey squirrels are larger than red squirrels and compete successfully for living space. At present the grey squirrels have spread from their original place of introduction at Castleforbes, Co. Longford, to colonise much of the east midlands and as far north as Co. Tyrone. The red squirrel has decreased in areas where the greys are well established but elsewhere they are doing well. There are no records of cross-breeding.

Apart from being larger, the grey squirrel has big rounded ears which lack the long tufts of the red squirrel's, and their fur is largely grey rather than red; but in winter the two species are more alike.

Red squirrels are found mainly in coniferous woodland and have benefited from the extensive plantations established this century. However, they do occur as well in deciduous woodland and hazel scrub. The grey squirrel is typical of mature deciduous woodland, parkland and estates. Both species are active by day and sleep at night in a nest called a drey. The grey squirrel's drey tends to be out on the branches of tall trees, while the red squirrel's is usually close to the trunk. Squirrels will also live in holes in trees and even birds' nests. Contrary to popular belief they do not hibernate but in cold winter weather they conserve energy by lying up in their dreys for long periods, emerging for a quick feed on warm days. Both squirrels eat a wide variety of mainly vegetable foods, including seeds, fruit, berries, nuts, fungi, bark and buds. They will also eat birds' eggs and nestlings, and insects. Red squirrels are fond of cones too. They will store food for the winter but often seem to forget where they have placed it.

Both species produce two litters of young each year, in early spring and in autumn, and the normal litter size is three or four. The young are born naked, blind and deaf but are weaned at 8 to 10 weeks and independent at 16 weeks. They can breed at 6 months but normally not until they are a year old. They do not mate for life.

	Head & Body	Tail	Weight
Grey Squirrel:	25-26 cm	21-22 cm	510 g full grown
Red Squirrel:	20-22 cm	17-18 cm	280 g full grown

The Crow (Rook in this story)

Corvus frugilegus   Rúcach

Strictly speaking, the term 'crow' should be used to indicate members of the crow family, the *Corvidae*, which includes ravens, hooded and carrion crows, rooks, jackdaws, magpies, jays and choughs. In this story the birds called crows are in fact rooks.

Rooks are common and widespread in Ireland and are largely resident here, though some may come to Ireland from Britain or the Continent in severe winters. They are large all-black birds about 50 cm from bill to tail and have broad wings with "fingered" feathers at the tips. When walking on the ground they appear to be wearing shaggy trousers. Close-up the black plumage has a glossy purple sheen. The adults have bare grey skin around the base of the bill where the feathers have been worn away by constant digging in the soil for worms, leather jackets and the like.

Rooks nest in colonies, known as rookeries, which are built on slender branches of tall trees, both deciduous and coniferous. Most building and repairing commences early in the spring and the young are often fledged by May or June. Usually 3-6 eggs are laid. These are greenish and mottled brown. Rookeries are noisy places with a constant sound of "cawing" birds.

The Badger

Meles meles   Broc

Badgers are usually rather shy and nocturnal creatures and therefore seldom seen. Sadly most people are familiar with them as traffic casualties on the roadside. Full grown they are sturdy heavy animals, measuring about 90 cm including a shortish tail and they weigh 10-12 kg (sometimes up to 17 or 18 kg). They are covered with rather coarse hair and have a grizzled grey appearance over most of the body, black underparts and feet, white head and a broad black band running from behind the nose through the eye and ear on each side. The female (sow) and male (boar) are very similar, while the young (cubs) are like small versions of their parents. Badgers live in sets which are a complex of underground passages with several entrances. These are excavated in deep soil deposits in sloping woodland and some sets have been used by generations of animals over hundreds of years. Badgers are very clean creatures and regularly turn out old bedding and replace it with new. From their sets badgers venture forth in dusk or darkness, relying on their keen sense of smell and hearing to detect danger (for their eyesight is weak) and to search for their food. They are omnivorous but are particularly fond of earthworms.

This species is native to Ireland and is common and widespread. They seldom do any harm to man's interest and yet in the past they were often mercilessly killed in badger-baiting and by gassing. The species is now fully protected by law. Recently there has been controversy about the role of badgers in harbouring bovine TB and reinfecting cattle with this disease. Research on this is currently in hand.

Badgers usually mate in the spring but sometimes as late as October. Embryo development does not begin until the following December or January. The cubs are born 8 weeks later and are weaned after 15 weeks. By the autumn they are three quarters grown and some wander away to take up life on their own, while others stay with their parents until the spring.

The Rat

Rattus norvegicus (brown rat)

Rattus rattus (black rat)   *Francach*

Two rat species are found in Ireland but neither is native. The black rat arrived first aboard ship in the Middle Ages but is now rare here and confined to a few sea ports. The brown rat (the species in this story) is a relative newcomer having arrived (again, aboard ship) probably in the early eighteenth century. They have successfully colonised all parts of Ireland even many remote and uninhabited islands. The brown rat is the larger of the two but has smaller ears, coarser fur and a thicker tail than the black rat and is a paler brown in colour. The brown rat grows to 28 cm excluding the tail which can double its length. Full grown rats normally weigh 150-200 g but individuals may reach 280 g.

Brown rats often associate closely with human habitations and can be a serious pest and carrier of disease both on the farm and in towns and cities. They consume large quantities of grain and also spoil stored cereals with their dropping. They are inveterate gnawers and have been known to gnaw holes through solid wood and even concrete. In summer many rats move away from homesteads and inhabit fields, hedgerows and embankments.

Rats usually live in colonies in extensive labyrinths of burrows in which they make their nesting chambers. This is lined with dry grass and other such material. They breed prolifically, the female giving birth to large litters (6-15) of young after only 24 days gestation. The young are tiny, blind and naked at birth but grow quickly and are weaned at about 3 weeks. Rats breed more or less continuously throughout the year if food is plentiful, and one female normally produces five litters in a year. It takes only 11 weeks for females to reach breeding age from birth.

The Swan

Cygnus olor (mute swan)

Cygnus cygnus (whopper swan)

Cygnus bewickii (Bewick's swan)   *Eala*

Three species of swan occur in Ireland: the resident mute swan (which is thought to have been introduced in early Norman times) and the migratory whooper and Bewick's swans which are winter visitors from (respectively) Iceland and Siberia. These migratory swans fly with silent wing beats but make loud trumpeting vocal calls. The mute swan utters snorts and hisses at times but is generally silent. In flight, however, they make a bell-like beating of their wings, trod with a lighter tread, as described by the poet W.B. Yeats. Whooper and Bewick's swans have black and bright yellow bills while the mutes have mainly orange bills, with a swollen fleshy black knob at the base. The young swans – cygnets – are pale greyish brown. The swans in this story are mute swans. Swans are our largest birds, measuring up to 150 cm and weighing sometimes 10-12 kg. They are so large and heavy they need plenty of room to take off from the water but once airborne are majestic fliers.

Mute swans do not usually breed until they are four years old. While immature they are gregarious and can be found sometimes in flocks, or herds, of several hundred. Breeding pairs, however, are highly territorial and can be very aggressive towards intruders. They will even stand their ground against humans when defending their nests, but there is no truth in the notion that they can break a man's leg with a blow from a wing. The nest is a huge mound of dead vegetation and 5-12 large pale green eggs are laid. The newly hatched cygnets often ride on the parents' backs in the water and they are cared for by the parents until the next breeding season when they are driven away.

Mute swans are common on waterways, lakes and large ponds throughout Ireland and are also found in estuaries and sheltered sea bays. They are vegetarian feeders and often become very tame when they are fed with bread crusts. Generally they do not wander far from their breeding areas. They have been known to live to twenty years in the wild.

The Fox

Vulpes vulpes   Madra rua/Sionnach

In general appearance foxes are like small dogs with long bushy tails held straight out behind. They normally grow to just over one metre in length, including the tail, and weigh six to seven kg (rarely up to 9 kg). The fur is reddish brown over most of the body but the tail is white-tipped and the lower muzzle and throat are also white. The ears are black on the rear side and foxes appear to be wearing blackish socks.

Foxes can be found almost everywhere from rich mixed farmland to forests, moors, high mountains and coastal habitats such as sand dunes and salt marshes. Increasingly they are found in suburbia and sometimes even in city parks and gardens where they often exist by scavenging from dustbins. Dens or sets are used mainly during the winter months and for rearing the young while in summer foxes often lie out on the suface in coverts or thickets. They enjoy basking in the sun in quiet places. While they will scavenge for food foxes are primarily carnivores and feed to a large